family picnic

ENDS

CLEVELAND
FEB 13
6 PM
STA. A

ST CARD

...tion

This space for Address only

...ft...

...ni...

...e c...

...ally thought...

... a local far...

...g basketbal...

...ot sure w...

...o great thi...

scholar... County. The...
Pfeffernut County. The...
...fernut had high hopes for Louie.

Lost Toys Returned

Townspeople are delighted by the surprising return of flying discs lost on rooftops and kites tangled high in treetops. Balls and other toys long since lost began to reappear in the yards of Pfeffernut County children a few weeks back. At first, no one knew just how these things were being returned from their high places. Then a local girl spotted a lanky farmhand named Louie as he plucked two baseballs from the gutters of her family's home.

"I couldn't believe my eyes," she said. "He's nearly as tall as the water tower."

"Aw, it's nothing," Louie said. "When I see those poor toys stuck where most folks can't reach, I feel real sorry. I can't help but reach down and put them back where they belong."

Please see LOUIE, Page A2

Greetings from
Pfeffernut County

Grandpa at
fishing hole

Pfeffernusse Cookies - 5 dozen

Grandma's recipe

4 C. flour
1/2 tsp. ground nutmeg
1/2 C. white sugar
3/4 C. light molasses
1 1/4 tsp. baking soda

1/2 C. butter
1/2 tsp. cinnamon
2 eggs
1/2 tsp. ground cloves
1/3 C. powdered sugar

Stir together flour, sugar, baking soda, spices + dash black pepper. Melt molasses + butter in saucepan. Cool. Stir in eggs, add dry ingredients to molasses mixture, mix well, cover. Chill for several hours. Shape into 1" balls. Place on cookie sheet. Bake at 350° 12 to 14 minutes or until cookies done. Cool. Roll in powdered s

The Cows Cannot Mooove Along

Pfeffernut County has not seen the sun for three straight days. Weather forecasters have no idea what's going on. The local livestock is completely frozen. Cows are no longer producing milk, just ice cream. Will this deep freeze continue, or will the sun shine down on Pfeffernut again?

Pfeffernut
Book Fair **$1**

Pfeffernut
Book Fair **$1**

FAWN BRAUN'S
Big City Blues

by Nick Healy

illustrated by Sahin Erkocak

PICTURE WINDOW BOOKS
Minneapolis, Minnesota

Special thanks to our story consultant:
Terry Flaherty, Ph.D., Professor of English
Minnesota State University, Mankato

Editor: Christianne Jones
Designer: Tracy Davies
Page Production: Melissa Kes
Art Director: Nathan Gassman
The illustrations in this book were
created digitally.

Picture Window Books
5115 Excelsior Boulevard
Suite 232
Minneapolis, MN 55416
877-845-8392
www.picturewindowbooks.com

Printed in the United States of America.

All books published by Picture Window Books
are manufactured with paper containing at
least 10 percent post-consumer waste.

Library of Congress Cataloging-in-Publication Data
Healy, Nick.
Fawn Braun's big city blues / by Nick Healy ; illustrated by
Sahin Erkocak.
p. cm. — (Pfeffernut County)
Summary: Fawn wants to leave her family's Pfeffernut County farm
and move to the big city as soon as she can and, in the meantime,
pretends she is already there, but her friend and neighbor Larry is
determined to keep her where she belongs.
ISBN-13: 978-1-4048-3696-9 (library binding)
ISBN-10: 1-4048-3696-9 (library binding)
[1. Farm life—Fiction. 2. Contentment—Fiction. 3. Friendship—
Fiction. 4. Tall tales.] I. Erkocak, Sahin, ill. II. Title.
PZ7.H34463Faw 2007
[E]—dc22
2007004032

To Helen and Erin – N.H.

WELCOME TO PFEFFERNUT

Pfeffernut County is a friendly little place on the prairie. It's full of kind people who dream big. Funny things have a way of happening here. Get ready for some new adventures, and enjoy your visit. We're sure glad you stopped by.

3

Fawn Braun was not fond of farm life. She did not like the mess. She did not like the smell. She did not like the flat fields and dusty roads.

Fawn's family lived in an old farmhouse on a dirt road. Most evenings, she stared out her bedroom window, watched the sun go down over the pasture, and heard cows moo in far-off places.

The nearest house stood clear across the field, so far away that Fawn could barely see it. Her neighbor, little Larry Flatland, lived there.

Fawn knew all about life in the big city.
She had learned it at the movies. Every
Saturday, Fawn went into town and
bought a ticket at the theater. Most times,
she brought along little Larry.

On the screen, lights shined on busy streets. Horns blared and traffic roared. People filled the sidewalks. They wore lovely dresses and handsome suits. They lived in tall towers, and at night, they could look out the window and see the whole big, beautiful place.

One Saturday, Fawn decided she would go to live in the city. She would wear fancy dresses and walk on busy sidewalks and live in a tall tower.

"That's it, Larry," she said. "I'm moving."

"What do you mean, Fawn Braun?" Larry asked. He liked to say her whole name. To him, it sounded like a little poem. "If you move, who will take me to the movies?"

Back home, Fawn told her parents about her plans.

"Don't be silly, Fawn," her father said.

"Dear," her mother said, "you should
be glad for what we have here."

"We don't have much," Fawn said. "We don't have tall buildings or taxicabs or tea parties. We don't have busy streets or bright lights or ballroom dances."

"But we have sunshine and fresh air," her mother said. "We have quiet nights and starlight."

But Fawn's mind was made up. If she couldn't move to the city, she would simply behave as though she lived there already.

"Gosh, Fawn Braun, where did you get those fancy clothes?" Larry asked at the bus stop. "Won't they get ruined at recess?"

"No time for recess," Fawn said. "I have a lunch date with the girls, and perhaps we'll stroll the grounds afterward."

Larry said, "Everyone has recess, Fawn Braun. It's the rule."

"You'll see," Fawn replied, placing a coin in the palm of the puzzled driver. "It's different for me."

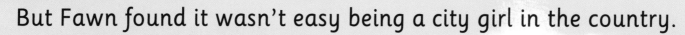

But Fawn found it wasn't easy being a city girl in the country.

Her heels got stuck in the mud.

Her gloves made milking difficult.

And there was never a taxicab when she needed one.

Soon Fawn gave up. She went back to her old clothes and her old way of life. But she was not happy about it.

"What's the matter, Fawn Braun?" Larry asked.

"I can't go to the city," Fawn replied. "And that makes me blue."

"You don't look blue," Larry said, squinting at his friend. "You look the same as ever."

"Not blue like the color," Fawn said. "Blue like sad."

21

Larry got right to work. He had an idea, a good one.

He went from shop to shop and door to door. He talked to everyone he knew—the old farmers, the man at the movie theater, the woman at the filling station, all the kids from school. Everyone.

He rounded up all the stuff he needed—old cans of paint, bunches of wire, and string after string of colored lights.

Fawn was still blue when the next Saturday came, but Larry wore a smile. When they walked out of the theater, the whole town had changed.

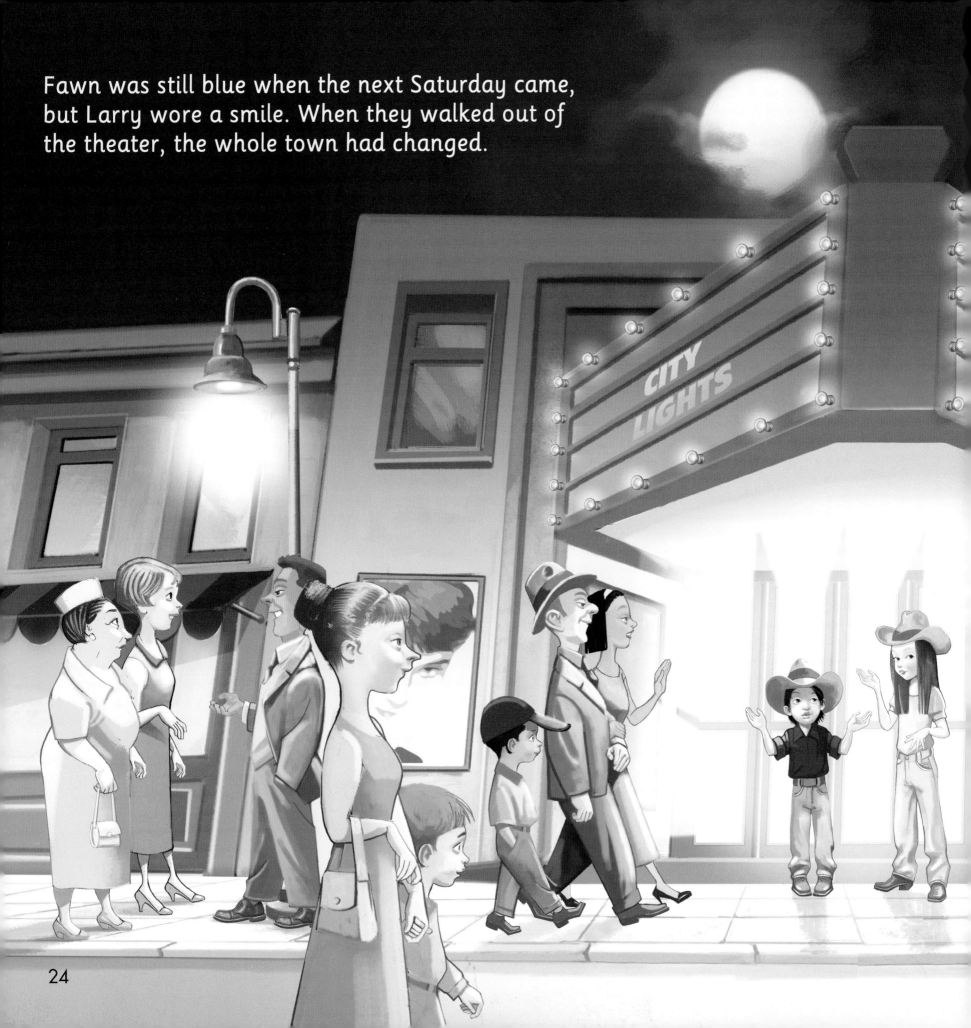

Old farmers blew their horns and waved as they drove down Main Street, which was clogged with traffic. The sidewalks were crowded, too. As people bustled by in fancy clothes, they smiled and said hello to Fawn.

Fawn and Larry had tea at a fancy sidewalk café.

And when they were finished, a taxicab
waited to whisk them home.

That night, cows mooed in far-off places as Fawn watched the sun go down over the pasture. The country was the same as always—until something amazing happened.

In the distance, a thousand lights flickered on and glowed in the darkness. They looked just like the lights of a faraway city.

Fawn smiled as she looked out at the whole big, beautiful place.

PFEFFERNUT FOLLOW-UP

1. Fawn wishes she could live in a big city, but her parents think life is nice in the country. What are some good things about life on the farm or in a small town?

2. Fawn likes going to the movies, and she learns from what she sees. What have you learned from movies? Do movies always show people and places the way they really are?

3. Do you ever wish you lived somewhere else? Where would it be? What makes your neighborhood a good place to live?

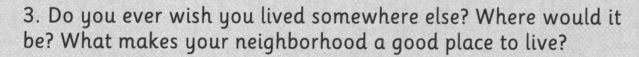

4. Larry doesn't want his friend to move away. He comes up with a plan to show her some fun in their small town. What else could he do to convince her that it's not such a bad place?

5. Have you ever felt like you didn't quite fit in? What did you do to get along? Did you get help from your friends or family?

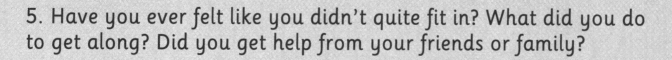

Fun Facts about city and country life

- In the early years, most citizens of the United States lived in the country. Nearly 95 of every 100 Americans lived in rural areas in 1790. Two hundred years later, most people—about three of every four—lived in urban areas, or cities.

- In 2000, the country's total population was about 281 million. About 59 million residents of the United States lived in rural areas. Rural areas include farmland and small towns.

- Tokyo, Japan, has more people than any other urban area in the world. New York City is the largest in the United States, while Toronto is the largest in Canada.

- The word fawn means a young deer.

- Fawn is also a name given to female children In the 1970s, it ranked 924th among names given to U.S. girls. Fawn has not made the list of the 1,000 most popular names since then.

The series title, "Pfeffernut County," comes from the German word *Pfeffernuesse* (FEFF-er-noos). Pfeffernuesse are German spice cookies that are popular around Christmastime. They get their spicy flavor from ingredients such as cinnamon, nutmeg, cloves, and black pepper.

50¢ weekdays $1.00 Sundays

More Books to Read

Barrett Judi. *Animals Should Definitely Not Wear Clothing.* New York: Aladdin Paperbacks, 2006.

Chall, Marsha Wilson. *Prairie Train.* New York: HarperCollins, 2003.

Falconer, Ian. *Olivia.* New York: Atheneum Books for Young Readers, 2000.

McMillan, Bruce. *The Problem with Chickens.* Boston: Houghton Mifflin Co., 2005.

Priceman, Marjorie. *How to Make an Apple Pie and See the World.* New York: Knopf, 1994.

FactHound

FactHound offers a safe, fun way to find Web sites related to topics in this book.

All of the sites on FactHound have been researched by our staff.

1. Visit *www.facthound.com*
2. Type in this special code: 1404836969
3. Click on the FETCH IT button.

Your trusty FactHound will fetch the best sites for you!

Look for all of the books in the Pfeffernut County series:

Farmer Cap
Fawn Braun's Big City Blues
Henry Shortbull Swallows the Sun
Louie the Layabout

Greetings from Pfeffernut County

Grandpa at fishing hole

Grandma's recipe

Pfeffernusse Cookies - 5 dozen

4 C. flour	½ C. butter
½ tsp. ground nutmeg	½ tsp. cinnamon
½ C. white sugar	2 eggs
¾ C. light molasses	½ tsp. ground cloves
1¼ tsp. baking soda	⅓ C. powdered sugar

Stir together flour, sugar, baking soda, spices + dash black pepper. Melt molasses + butter in saucepan. Cool.

Stir in eggs, add dry ingredients to molasses mixture, mix well, cover, chill for several hours. Shape into 1" balls. Place on cookie sheet. Bake at 350° until 12 to 14 minutes or until cookie done. Cool. Roll in powdered s...

The Cows Cannot Mooove Along

Pfeffernut County has not seen the sun for three straight days. Weather forecasters have no idea what's going on. The local livestock is completely frozen. Cows are no longer producing milk, just ice cream. Will this deep freeze continue, or will the sun shine down on Pfeffernut again?

Pfeffernut Book Fair $1

Pfeffernut Book Fair $1

PFEFFERNUT

harvest time

School Book Drive a Colorful Success!

A small bet between the principal and students at Pfeffernut Elementary School has led to the largest book drive in the school's history. The students collected 1,000 books in just one week.

"We challenged our students, and they made us proud," the principal said. "Now I have to fulfill my part of the bet and dye my hair blue for the rest of the school year."

Pfeffernut Theater Grand Reopening

Downtown Pfeffernut looked more like New York City than a small town on Friday night. Bright lights glared, loud music blared, and huge crowds poured into the local theater to celebrate its grand reopening.

Main Street, minutes befo...

Last summer, a huge tornado destroyed the theater. Staying true to

Pfeffernut form, t... fitting movie to be "Twister." Pleas...

...urmer Gets ...License

...ap of Pfeffernut ...lured many hours in

F R